Fish Fingers
and Leaks

First published in 2011
by Wayland

This edition published in 2014

Text copyright © Tom Easton
Illustration copyright © Matt Buckingham

Wayland
338 Euston Road
London NW1 3BH

Wayland Australia
Level 17/207 Kent Street
Sydney, NSW 2000

Series Editor: Louise John
Editor: Katie Woolley
Cover design: Paul Cherrill
Design: D.R.ink
Consultant: Shirley Bickler

A CIP catalogue record for this book is available from the British Library.

ISBN 9780750264952

Printed in China

3 5 7 9 10 8 6 4

Wayland is a division of Hachette Children's Books,
an Hachette UK Company

www.hachette.co.uk

Fish Fingers and Leaks

Written by Tom Easton
Illustrated by Matt Buckingham

WAYLAND

Captain Flint and the Poor Pirates were very happy. They'd just got hold of a Spanish fishing boat and they had stolen a big sack of fish fingers!

Long John and his parrot were doing the cooking.

While the pirates waited, Captain Flint
told Arthur to go down to the hold and
see if there was any ketchup.

When Arthur got into the hold,
he didn't find any ketchup. He found
something else – a leak!

They all went down to have a look.

"We need to stop it, Captain," Selma
pointed out, "or else the Stuck Pig
will sink."

"Does anyone have any ideas?" the Captain asked.

"We could stick a cork in the hole," Selma said.

"Where can we get a cork from?"
growled Big Ben.

"From one of the Captain's barrels
of rum," Selma said, matter of factly.

"I really don't think that's a good idea," pointed out the Captain. "After all, the rum would leak out and we're trying to stop leaks, not start new ones."

At last, the Captain clicked his fat
fingers and laughed.

"I've had a **brilliant** idea," he said.
"Arthur, stick your finger in the hole."

Arthur did as he was told.
He wondered what the Captain's
brilliant idea would be.

"Right, that's stopped the leak," said the Captain. "Let's go and see if the fish fingers are done."

"That **is** a brilliant idea," Pegleg Pete said.

Up on deck, the pirates sat down at the table. Suddenly Arthur popped his head up through the hatch.

"You're supposed to be stopping that leak!" the Captain roared, angrily.

"I was," Arthur replied, "but now there's another leak and I can't reach both at once."

The Captain sighed and rolled his eyes. "Selma, get down there and block the other leak."

Selma and Arthur were very grumpy about having to block the leaks and miss out on the fish fingers.

"I really like fish fingers," Arthur said, his tummy rumbling.

When another leak started up,
Selma stomped back up on deck
to tell the Captain.

A grumpy Pegleg Pete came down and
jammed his wooden leg into the big hole.

"How are those fish fingers coming along?" the Captain called. "I'm starving."

"Squawk! Nearly done, Captain," said Long John's parrot.

"Captain!" cried Pegleg Pete.
"There's another leak."

This time Big Ben had to go and plug
the leak. It was a very big hole and poor
old Ben had to sit on it.

All the pirates were very glum indeed.
They could smell the fish fingers cooking
up on deck and their mouths watered.

The Captain was glum, too.
"Looks like I'll be eating dinner on my
own tonight," he said to himself.

Just then Long John came over carrying the fish fingers.

"Hurrah!" shouted the Captain, forgetting all about his crew.

Suddenly there was a shout from below.

"Leak!" cried the four pirates in the hold.

"Off you go, Long John," the Captain
said to the cook, who had just sat down.

"Make that two leaks," came
another cry.

"You'd better go, too," the Captain said
to Long John's parrot.

Now there were five pirates and a parrot in the hold, all plugging the leaks.

"Why isn't the Captain down here helping us?" Selma said.

"It's not fair that he gets to eat fish fingers without us," Arthur added.

"Squawk! We should have just let the Stuck Pig sink," said Long John's parrot.

"Yeah," said Big Ben. "That would teach the Captain a lesson."

Just then the Captain arrived carrying a huge tray.

"Don't worry, I've got the fish fingers!"
the Captain boomed, as he handed
them out. "These will do the trick!"

"Captain?" Selma asked, looking at the empty tray, then at the fish fingers plugging the leaks. "I thought you'd brought the fish fingers for us to eat!"

"To eat?" replied the Captain. "I'm surprised at you, Selma, thinking of your stomach when the ship's in danger!"

The Captain shook his head sadly and gave a little burp.

START READING is a series of highly enjoyable books for beginner readers. **The books have been carefully graded to match the Book Bands widely used in schools.** This enables readers to be sure they choose books that match their own reading ability.

Look out for the Band colour on the book in our Start Reading logo.

The Bands are:

Pink Band 1A & 1B

Red Band 2

Yellow Band 3

Blue Band 4

Green Band 5

Orange Band 6

Turquoise Band 7

Purple Band 8

Gold Band 9

START READING books can be read independently or shared with an adult. They promote the enjoyment of reading through satisfying stories, plays and non-fiction narratives, which are supported by fun illustrations and photographs.

Tom Easton lives in Surrey, works in London and spends a lot of time travelling between the two, which is when he does his writing. Tom has written books for children, teenagers and adults, under a variety of pseudonyms. He has three children and is looking forward to having macaroni cheese tonight.

Matt Buckingham would have rather liked a job as a pirate if he hadn't become an illustrator. The only problem is Matt gets seasick, so it's probably best if he sticks to drawing pirates instead.